THINGS THAT WOULD BE COOLER

➔ →COOLER← ←

WITH

ZAZER BEAMS

KITTENS

Mee ouch!

BIKES

BUTTERFLYS

Pencils

ANTS

HUMMINGBIRDS

(Hmmmmm zap!)

TADPOLES

ME !!!

...IONS ...RED

OF

WAITING

FOR

GRAVITY SHOES

I MEAN COME ON!
WHATS SO TOUGH
ABOUT THAT? !!!

JET PACKS!

SO I've
been
ready for
this since like
kindergarden......

MACHINE
that
makes
CRUMMY
FOODS
that you
are forced
to eat
TASTE
LIKE
BACON !!!

I need this now.

brossel sprouts?
No problem! Tastes like
bacon!!!

Billy's Booger

A MEMOIR (which is a true story, which this book is)

WRITTEN AND DRAWN by

WILLIAM JOYCE

AND HIS YOUNGER SELF (from the 4th grade, actually)

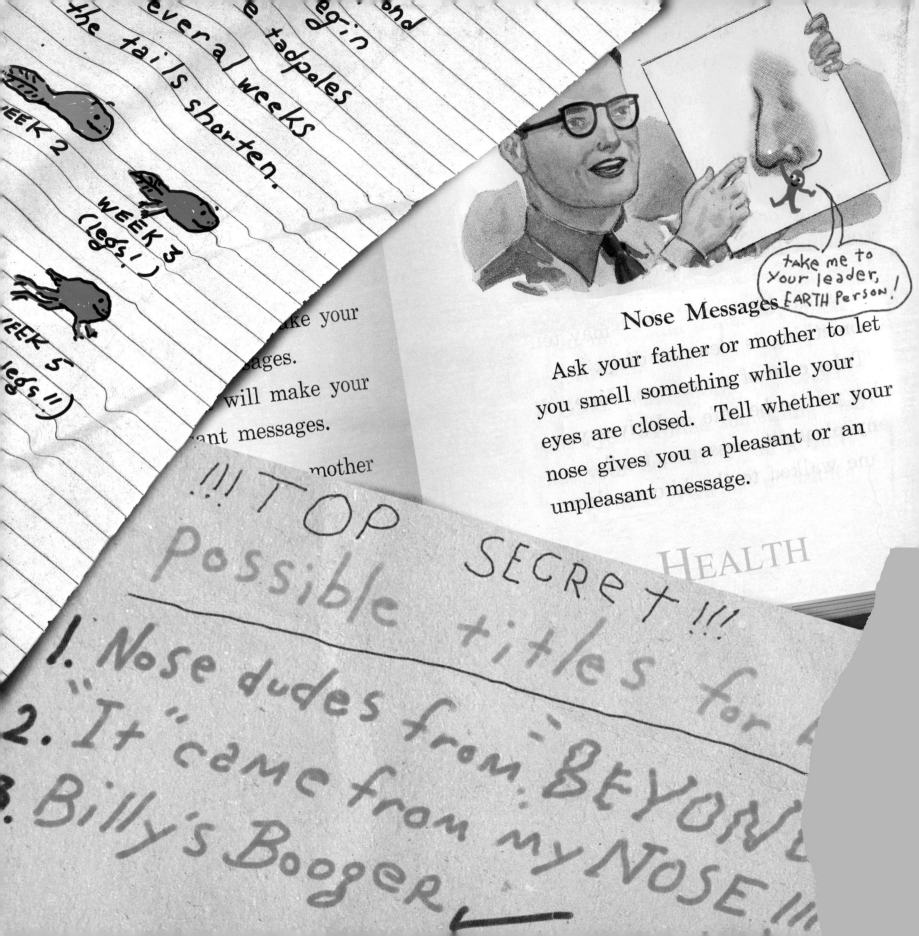

WEEK 2

WEEK 3
(legs!)

WEEK 5
(legs!!)

the tails shorten.

several weeks

tadpoles

begin

make your

...ages.

will make your

...ant messages.

mother

Nose Messages

Ask your father or mother to let you smell something while your eyes are closed. Tell whether your nose gives you a pleasant or an unpleasant message.

take me to your leader, EARTH Person!

HEALTH

!!! TOP SECRET !!!

Possible titles for

1. Nose dudes from BEYOND
2. "It came from my NOSE!!!"
3. Billy's Booger

Once upon a time, when TV was in black and white, and there were only three channels, and when kids didn't have playdates—they just roamed free in the "out of doors"—there lived a kid named Billy.

Billy loved monster movies and cartoons and comic books and something called "the funny papers." During the week, the "funnies" were small and in black and white, but on Sundays they were huge and in color, and if you spread them all out, they would fill a room.

Billy wished school was more like the funny papers, but his efforts at making math more fun were not entirely successful.

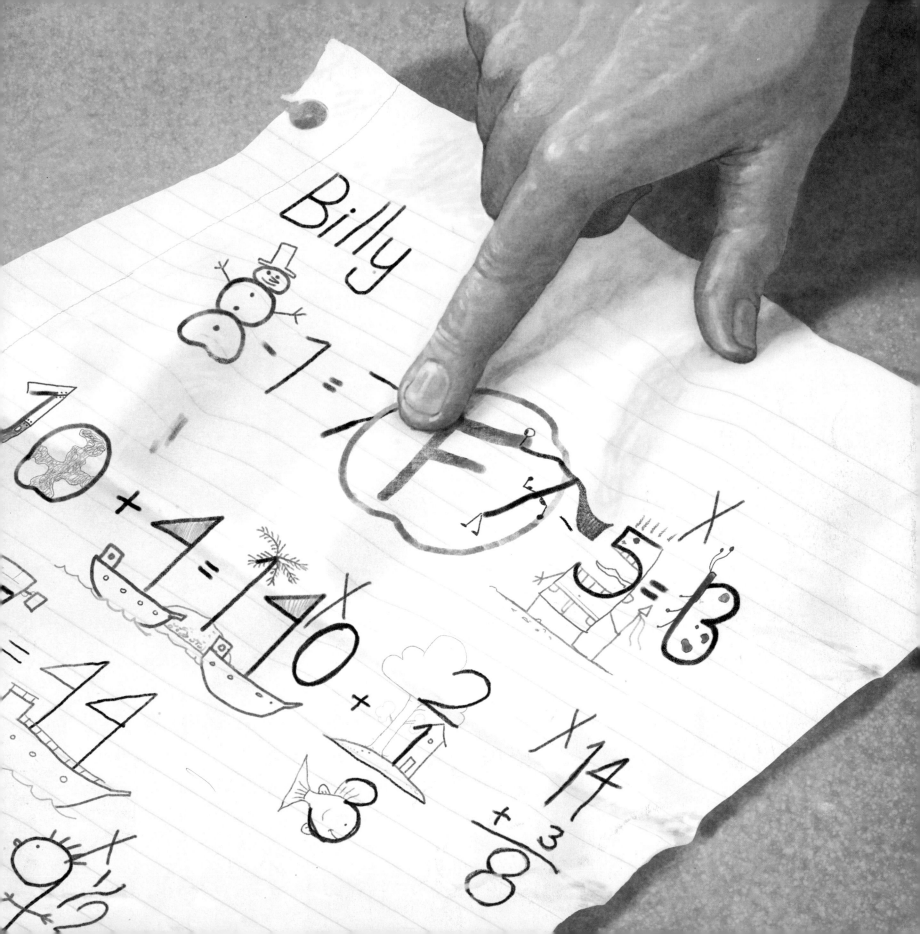

Billy also found regular sports too regular.

He did much better at sports he invented.

But the PE teacher didn't entirely agree.

Every now and then, Billy would get sent home from school with A NOTE, but his parents always wrote back: "Ahh! You should see the stuff he does at home!"

Dear Mr. & Mrs. Billy,

Your son has been very odd as of late. And while we always try to encourage creativity, we cannot condone full-fledged ... and mayhem.

... osition

Then one day, Mrs. Pagely, the librarian, announced there would be a contest to see which kid could make the best kids' book. Billy's brain was about to explode! He asked the librarian for books on many different subjects. "Meteors, mythology, space travel, and mucus!"

"What have I done?" Mrs. Pagely worried.

Book Contest

The books will be judged in these categories:

Neatness.. 10 Possible Points
Spelling.. 10 Possible Points
Vocabulary.. 10 Possible Points
Punctuation.. 10 Possible Points
Grammar.. 10 Possible Points
Imagination.. 10 Possible Points

For the next few days, Billy thought and read and wrote and drew.

"Well, his nose is certainly to the grindstone," said Billy's dad.

"I wonder what kind of note he'll get this time?" said his sister.

But Billy didn't hear them. He was living the dream.

The name of his book?

Billy's Booger

The memoir of a little green nose buddy.

Chapter 1.
I am Sneezed

I was just a regular booger inside the regular nose of a regular kid named Billy.

All the other boogers were there. Nick & Ed on the left. Me and Curley on the right. We were watchin' Billy do his math.

4+7=

SAD

Billy →

we are here

Billy went "exploring" So we
had to hide.
"He's been biting his nails again."
said curly.
"must Be a math test comin' up"
said Ed
"Too bad we can't help him"
                              I said.

Right then, way way way in outer space a star sneezed and out came this metorite that zoomed all the way to earth and through Billys window !!!

SPACE

OUTER

Achoooooo!

Look out below !!!

♪♪ sniffle !
Sniffle
Little
star ♫

SATURN

EARTH
↓
(our planet)

USA

Billys
house

The metorite bonked Billy
RIGHT ON the TOP of his
HEAD!!!! We were all knocked
out "cold."
Then Billy   sNeezed and out
I came

BONK!!

ACHOO!!!!

me

Chapter 2
"Super Booger"

When we woke up I had incredible math =powers= and was green Really Really GREEN and I decided that I would use my POWERZ to help poor Billy out.

KNOT ON head

Though only a booger I will help you become the worlds greatest mathmatical genius!!!

gee thanks you are my pal and a super Booger!

$E = MC^2$

$2\sqrt{50}$

Well, the name "SUPER BOOGER" stuck
I was faster than a speeding spitball

← me

MORE POWerful than the meaniest
bully!

Heelp!

ABLe to Leap tall swingsets with
a single sneeze

Achooo !!!

Then Billy started getting
amazing and totally dif-
green peas into chocolate. And he
could ware a cape) And he ~~was~~ could be in-
teresting all at the same time....

ugg! Peas!!

Don't worry
I'll use my
chocolate
Ray vision!

→ Super Powers that were
→ erent from mine He could turn
→ could Fly (which of course ment he
→ visible! AND generally super in—

where r u Billy?

Right here!!!
reciting the en-
cyclopedia backwards

ZYZZA
a genus of
grass-
hoppers!

AND WITH MY HELP, Billy could do the hardest math any teacher ever taught. Even the PRESIDENT asked Billy math advise.

Chapter 3

And sooo Billy became the "go to" kid on the whole darned planet when it came to math stoff and Bad Guys, and super Villians and Crime. Nick and Ed and Curley just stayed Nose-side (they got gyped on the super powers)

BUT.... wheneverever the need arrived I'd blast out of Billys Nose and we would SAVE THE DAY !! !!

we're ok with that... REALLY

BANG!!!

"OUT OUT and AWAY!!!"

(our motto.)

THE END....?

Dont bet on it!!!!!

Pubished in USA by Billy © blah blah blah

done entirely in green pens and 1 white pencil

XII V 3 007

Principal Blisterbaum would be the judge

for the contest.

Billy liked the principal. He got sent to him all the time.

Especially during the science fair. He called Billy

"one of my most challenging students ever." So the day

the winners were announced, Billy was pretty excited.

But . . .

He didn't win first place.

He didn't win second place.

He didn't win third place.

He didn't get an honorable mention.

He didn't get a note from his teacher.

He didn't even get sent to the principal.

It was a long walk home.

His mom and dad were concerned about him.

Even his sister was worried. "Billy is so normal now,

it's weird."

A week or so later, Billy glumly took all the library books back. Even the ones about mucus. Mrs. Pagely smiled at him in a nutty sort of way. Then Billy heard laughing.

Some of his friends and some older kids were at
a table reading a book.

"This is hilarious!"

"I wanna check this out next."

"This book shoulda won SOMETHING!"

"I put all the contest books in the library," said Mrs. Pagely.

"But yours is checked out the most, Billy."

He hadn't won first. Or second. Or third. Or an honorable mention. But his book was now in the library. And it was checked out the most.

This made Billy smile.

In a Billy sort of way.

"You got a twenty in Imagination," said one of Billy's pals. But Billy didn't hear him. His mind was on fire. He wasn't so normal it was weird anymore, and he was still Mr. Blisterbaum's most challenging student.

Book Contest

Entry: Billy's _____ger

Neatness.......... 10 Possible Points 3
Spelling............ 10 Possible Points 3 Terrible though inventive
Vocabulary...... 10 Possible Points 4 Extremely inventive
Punctuation.... 10 Possible Points 3 Pull back on the "!"s.
Grammar.......... 10 Possible Points 6 BIZARRE
Imagination.....10 Possible Points 20 !!!!! No problem there.
As usual

TOTAL 39

Comments:

Work on those low scores, Billy.
I look forward to what you come
up with next year.

Mr. Blisterbaum

PS You're still my most
challenging student

And the walk home?

It was just the beginning . . .

of a long,

long

adventure.